Damon and the Magic Christmas Tree

illustrated by:
Ebony Glenn

written by:
Tash Creates

To all of my beautiful nieces and nephews

Damon loves superheroes and wants nothing more than the Superman action figure for Christmas. For the first time, Damon and his family—mother, Natalie; father, Seth; and sister, Elizabeth, Lizzie for short—will not celebrate Christmas in Seattle, because they are going to spend the holidays with his grandma in New York City.

Damon would rather stay in Seattle, close to home, friends, and everything he knows.

Damon's teacher, Mrs. Smith, asked the class to share their plans for the holiday break.

Damon raises his hand high to express his dismay. "Well, my parents are making me go to New York."

Mrs. Smith replies, "That's great, Damon! There is a magic tree there."

"A magic tree?!" he continues. "What magic tree?"

"The annual tree-lighting ceremony is in Rockefeller Center. The tree is over one hundred feet tall," Mrs. Smith adds.

"What is Rockefeller Center?" Damon inquires further.

"Rockefeller Center is a place for people coming together for community celebrations of the arts, culture, music, and the famous tree-lighting ceremony every winter."

Damon didn't wait for the bell. Seconds before it sounds, he runs to the school bus anxious to get home.

Damon's parents, Natalie and Seth, come out to greet their excited son. The rainy winter day was calming and peaceful, until Damon bombarded them with questions.

"Mom, is it true. Is it true?"

"Is what true, Damon?"

"Is there a magic tree?!Well, is there?"

"Damon, let's go inside." Damon takes off his rain boots and rests his umbrella and jacket on the hook near the front door.

Damon jumps on his father's lap and awaits the answers to his questions.

Natalie begins, "There is a tree that stands one hundred feet tall. It is decorated in beautiful bulbs, ornaments, and lights so bright they light up the whole city. It's like magic." He is told again about this magic tree.

He repeats, "Like Magic," before going to play with his toys for an hour before supper.

Later on that night, after a mug of hot chocolate, Damon dreams of this giant tree.

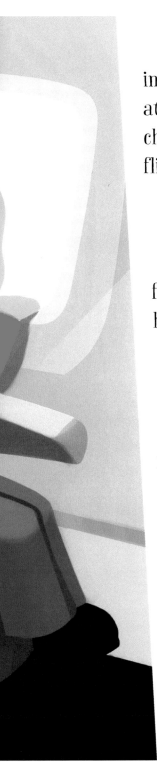

The next day Damon leans back into his chair and the flight attendant brings him a cup of hot chocolate. He leans over to see the flight takeoff.

"Are you excited, Damon?"

"Yes, I can't wait!"

As the flight took off, the Cohen family said good-bye to Seattle and hello to New York.

A taxi drops Damon and his family off to a tall brick building.

"What's here, Mommy? Why are we stopping?"

"Damon, this is where your grandmother lives."

"Grandma lives here?"

Damon's father removes the last piece of luggage from the trunk of the taxi cab.

"Come on, Damon. Let's go see your granny. She has wanted to see you for so long."

Damon, unsure of himself and his surroundings, follows his parents into the old brick building, up the elevator to apartment 1127.

Knock. Knock.

"Who is it?"

"It's Seth, your son."

A short, gray-haired woman opens the door. She is all smiles, and Damon's worries cease for the moment.

"Damon, you're so big. Give Granny a hug."

Damon walks up to cuddle with his granny. She smells of cinnamon and nutmeg.

"Come on in, make yourselves at home. I've got some cider in the kitchen and supper is almost ready. Seth, your sister, nieces and nephews are in the other room."

Damon looks around the small apartment and notices there is not a tree in sight. He sees a long table and on top of it is a stand with nine lit candles.

"Where's the Christmas tree, Mommy?"

"They do not celebrate Christmas in this household. They'll be celebrating Hanukkah."

"What's Hanukkah?" A sad look crosses Damon's face. First no tree in sight, and now, no Christmas.

Damon asked, "How can you be so happy without Christmas? I don't see Christmas anywhere here."

Caitlin, his oldest girl cousin responds, "Christmas isn't about what you see or receive. It is about what you give and share with others."

14

"What do you mean give and share with others?" Damon is confused.

"Giving love could be as simple as giving a hug to the people you love and sharing the joy for the life God has given you, us all."

Damon, confused, says, "Hugs and love are not gifts."

"Says who? They are in Granny's house."

Caitlin begins to tickle Damon. Damon can't help but to burst into uncontrollable laughter.

"Come, sit around me," Granny says.

All of the grandkids sit around their grandmother. They are snuggled up in their blankets and dressed in their pajamas.

"I couldn't help but overhear you earlier, Damon, about not celebrating Christmas."

Damon looks down.

"Look at me, Damon. There is no need to be embarrassed. We celebrate God's love here. I know at home you're used to getting everything you want, but this is your home too."

"It is?"

"Yes, home is where the heart is and the heart is always with family."

"Is that true what you said?" Damon asks his grandmother, who is sitting beside his cot.

"Yes, Damon, home is where the heart is. You're a part of me and I am a part of you and that's why even though you live in Seattle and I in New York, we are never that far away because our hearts keep us close."

His grandmother tells him a story of Hanukkah.

"The hanukkiyah is lit every night for eight nights and we spin the dreidel." His grandmother shows Damon a photo of the menorah and game.

"We commemorate the oil to rededicate ourselves to God, our creator."

Damon smiled and snuggled up in his blanket before falling fast asleep.

The next morning, Damon wakes up excited! It is nine hours until the tree-lighting ceremony.

"Good morning, Damon, did you sleep okay?"

"Yes, Mommy, I did. Guess what is going to happen in eight hours and fifty-six minutes?"

"What?"

"The magic tree is going to light up!"

"You're absolutely right. Well, we better have some breakfast and get you dressed for this amazingly magical day."

Natalie, Seth, Lizzie and, Damon head out to sight see New York City. The last stop on their agenda for the day is Rockefeller Center.

"Where are we off to now, daddy? It is 5:30."
"Oh you're right, Damon. Let's head toward Rockefeller Center."

"Yes!" Damon screams in excitement. "I can't wait."

"Oh, wait let me get this. I don't recognize this number." Seth answers his phone and the look on his face warns that something may be wrong.

The person on the other line says, "Is this Seth Cohen?"

"Yes, this is Seth Cohen? What's wrong?"

"Your mother was brought into New York Hospital Queens thirty minutes ago."

Seth quietly thanks the nurse and hangs up.

"We have to go see Grandma. I'm sorry, Damon, but your grandmother is not well."

"Okay," Damon replies disappointedly. Suddenly he realizes what this means.

"Does this mean we will not see the magic tree?"

"I'm afraid not, honey. Let's go."

They head to the hospital to see Grandma.

"Right this way, she's doing great." A nurse assures the family

"Hi, Grandma! What are you doing in here?"

"Oh, Damon, old age I suppose. Look what've I got on TV for you."

Natalie begins to sing, "Silent night, holy night, all has come, all is bright, round young virgin, mother and child, holy infant, so tender and mild..."

"Look Damon, they're counting down: 5, 4, 3, 2, 1." His grandmother taps him to make him focus on the big TV screen.

Seconds after the countdown was over, the magic tree lit up and spread light throughout the city.

Everyone cheered and gave hugs and kisses to one another. Damon smiles at his grandmother and says, "Happy holidays."

"Happy holidays, Damon, happy holidays."

It is Christmas Eve and Damon can hardly fall sleep. "Finally, it's Christmas!" Damon says excitedly while waking up.

"Merry Christmas, Damon, this is from me and your dad." Inside of the gift box is the Superman action figure.

"Thank you." Damon is grateful, but looks down.

Suddenly the front door to the apartment opens, it is Grandma Kate.

"Grandma, Grandma!" Damon runs to greet and hug his grandmother.

"You're home."

"I'm home, this is for you." In her hands is a tiny gift box. She hands it to Damon. He slowly opens it. Inside is a tiny tree that lights up and plays Christmas carols.

"It's like magic." Damon says smiling.

Until next time, tell someone that you love them.

Made in the USA
Monee, IL
21 December 2019